The Perfect Pet

by Courtney Baker
Illustrated by Jackie Snider

Hello Reader! — Level 1

SCHOLASTIC INC.
New York Toronto London Auckland Sydney
Mexico City New Delhi Hong Kong Buenos Aires

Some pets are small.

Some pets are big.

To my parents,
Howard and Carolyn
—C.B.

For Ellen, Delia, Kim, Tina, Laura, and Marley.
Good friends, Dressage divas,
and the best Perfect Pet moms.
—J.S.

ISBN 0-439-47111-7

12 11 10 8/0

Printed in the U.S.A. • First printing, March 2003
Book design by Janet Kusmierski

Dear Family and Friends of Young Readers,

Learning to read is one of the most important milestones your child will ever attain. Early reading is hard work, but you can make it easier with Hello Readers.

Just like learning to play a sport or an instrument, learning to read requires many opportunities to work on skills. However, you have to get in the game or experience real music to keep interested and motivated. Hello Readers are carefully structured to provide the right level of text for practice and great stories for experiencing the fun of reading.

Try these activities:

- Reading starts with the alphabet and at the earliest level, you may encourage your child to focus on the sounds of letters in words and sounding out words. With more experienced readers, focus on how words are spelled. Be word watchers!
- Go beyond the book — talk about the story, how it compares with other stories, and what your child likes about it.
- Comprehension — did your child get it? Have your child retell the story or answer questions you may ask about it.

Another thing children learn to do at this age is learn to ride a bike. You put training wheels on to help them in the beginning and guide the bike from behind. Hello Readers help you support your child and then you get to watch them take off as skilled readers.

— Francie Alexander
Chief Academic Officer
Scholastic Education

Some pets are quiet.

Some pets are loud.

Some people like to watch their pets.

Some people like to play with their pets.

Today, my family will get a pet.

I wonder what it will be?

My sister wants a pet
with spots.
She wants to show it off to
her friends.

My brother wants a fluffy pet.
He wants to be able to hold it.

I want a pet that I can play with!

I ask Dad what kind of pet

he wants.

He does not know.

"I'm sure we'll find the perfect pet at the store," he says.

I tell Mom about the pet I want.

"Your pet sounds very nice!"

she says. "But your sister and

brother must agree."

I am worried.

Will we be able to find the

perfect pet?

I try to think of a pet that
we will all like.
It has to be fluffy and playful.
It must have spots.

Yikes! That looks more like

a monster than a pet!

It's time to choose our pet.

We get into the car.

Away we go!

At the pet store, my sister sees
a lizard in a tank.
"A lizard is the perfect pet!"
she says.

“Let’s keep looking,” Dad says.

My brother sees a rabbit

in a cage.

"A rabbit is the perfect pet!"

he says.

"Let's wait and see," Mom says.

There! In the pen! Two brown eyes peek out at us.

"A puppy!" I shout. "A puppy is the perfect pet for all of us!"

My sister and brother agree.

Hooray! We have a new puppy!

Our puppy likes to play.

We run races.

We roll in the grass.

When we are tired, we take naps together.

He is our best friend.

We take care of him.

We give him food and water.

He gets a treat when he is good.

My sister likes to show her friends the tricks our puppy learns.

My brother is happy because our puppy is small and soft.

We agree — our puppy is the perfect pet!